Kate Douglas Wiggin

The birds' Christmas carol

Kate Douglas Wiggin

The birds' Christmas carol

ISBN/EAN: 9783743306202

Manufactured in Europe, USA, Canada, Australia, Japa

Cover: Foto ©Andreas Hilbeck / pixelio.de

Manufactured and distributed by brebook publishing software
(www.brebook.com)

Kate Douglas Wiggin

The birds' Christmas carol

THE BIRDS' CHRISTMAS CAROL.

"THE LITTLE RUGGLESES BORE IT BRAVELY." Page 42.

THE BIRDS' CHRISTMAS CAROL

BY

KATE DOUGLAS WIGGIN

BOSTON AND NEW YORK
HOUGHTON, MIFFLIN AND COMPANY
The Riverside Press, Cambridge
1889

The Riverside Press, Cambridge:
Electrotyped and Printed by H. O. Houghton & Co.

To

The Three Dearest Children in the World,

BERTHA, LUCY, AND HORATIO.

" O little ones, ye cannot know
The power with which ye plead,
Nor why, as on through life we go,
The little child doth lead."

CONTENTS AND LIST OF ILLUSTRATIONS.

The Birds' Christmas Carol.

I.

IT was very early Christmas morning, and in the stillness of the dawn, with the soft snow falling on the housetops, a little child was born in the Bird household.

They had intended to name the baby Lucy, if it were a girl; but they hadn't expected her on Christmas morning, and a real Christmas baby was not to be lightly named—the whole family agreed in that.

They were consulting about it in the nursery. Mr. Bird said that he had assisted in naming the three boys, and that he should leave this matter entirely to Mrs. Bird; Donald wanted the child called "Maud," after a pretty little curly-haired girl who sat next him in school; Paul chose "Luella," for Luella was the nurse who had been with him during his whole

babyhood, up to the time of his first trousers, and the
name suggested all sorts of comfortable things.   Uncle
Jack said that the first girl should always be named for
her mother, no matter how hideous the name happened
to be.

Grandma said that she would prefer not to take any
part in the discussion, and everybody suddenly remembered that Mrs. Bird had thought of naming the baby
Lucy, for Grandma herself; and, while it would be
indelicate for her to favor that name, it would be
against human nature for her to suggest any other,
under the circumstances.

Hugh, the "hitherto baby," if that is a possible
term, sat in one corner and said nothing, but felt, in
some mysterious way, that his nose was out of joint;
for there was a newer baby now, a possibility he had
never taken into consideration; and the "first girl,"
too, a still higher development of treason, which made
him actually green with jealousy.

But it was too profound a subject to be settled then
and there, on the spot; besides, Mama had not been
asked, and everybody felt it rather absurd, after all,
to forestall a decree that was certain to be absolutely
wise, just and perfect.

The reason that the subject had been brought up at all so early in the day lay in the fact that Mrs. Bird never allowed her babies to go over night unnamed. She was a person of so great decision of character that she would have blushed at such a thing; she said that to let blessed babies go dangling and dawdling about without names, for months and months, was enough to ruin them for life. She also said that if one could not make up one's mind in twenty-four hours it was a sign that—but I will not repeat the rest, as it might prejudice you against the most charming woman in the world.

So Donald took his new velocipede and went out to ride up and down the stone pavement and notch the shins of innocent people as they passed by, while Paul spun his musical top on the front steps.

But Hugh refused to leave the scene of action. He seated himself on the top stair in the hall, banged his head against the railing a few times, just by way of uncorking the vials of his wrath, and then subsided into gloomy silence, waiting to declare war if more "first girl babies" were thrust upon a family already surfeited with that unnecessary article.

Meanwhile dear Mrs. Bird lay in her room, weak, but

safe and happy with her sweet girl baby by her side and the heaven of motherhood opening before her. Nurse was making gruel in the kitchen, and the room was dim and quiet. There was a cheerful open fire in the grate, but though the shutters were closed, the side windows that looked out on the Church of our Saviour, next door, were wide open.

Suddenly a sound of music poured out into the bright air and drifted into the chamber. It was the boy-choir singing Christmas anthems. Higher and higher rose the clear, fresh voices, full of hope and cheer, as children's voices always are. Fuller and fuller grew the burst of melody as one glad strain fell upon another in joyful harmony:

> " Carol, brothers, carol,
>   Carol joyfully,
>   Carol the good tidings,
>   Carol merrily!
>   And pray a gladsome Christmas
>   For all your fellow-men;
>   Carol, brothers, carol,
>   Christmas Day again."

One verse followed another always with the same glad refrain:

'And pray a gladsome Christmas
For all your fellow-men:
Carol, brothers, carol,
Christmas Day again.''

Mrs. Bird thought, as the music floated in upon her gentle sleep, that she had slipped into heaven with her new baby, and that the angels were bidding them welcome. But the tiny bundle by her side stirred a little, and though it was scarcely more than the ruffling of a feather, she awoke; for the mother-ear is so close to the heart that it can hear the faintest whisper of a child.

She opened her eyes and drew the baby closer. It looked like a rose dipped in milk, she thought, this pink and white blossom of girlhood, or like a pink cherub, with its halo of pale yellow hair, finer than floss silk.

" Carol, brothers, carol,
Carol joyfully,
Carol the good tidings,
Carol merrily!"

The voices were brimming over with joy.

" Why, my baby," whispered Mrs. Bird in soft surprise, "I had forgotten what day it was. You are a little Christmas child, and we will name you 'Carol'— mother's little Christmas Carol!"

" What!" said Mr. Bird, coming in softly and closing the door behind him.

" Why, Donald, don't you think 'Carol' is a sweet name for a Christmas baby? It came to me just a moment ago in the singing as I was lying here half asleep and half awake."

" I think it is a charming name, dear heart, and that it sounds just like you, and I hope that, being a girl, this baby has some chance of being as lovely as her mother," at which speech from the baby's papa, Mrs. Bird, though she was as weak and tired as she could be, blushed with happiness.

And so Carol came by her name.

Of course, it was thought foolish by many people, though Uncle Jack declared laughingly that it was very strange if a whole family of Birds could not be indulged in a single Carol; and Grandma, who adored the child, thought the name much more appropriate than Lucy, but was glad that people would probably think it short for Caroline.

Perhaps because she was born in holiday time, Carol was a very happy baby. Of course, she was too tiny to understand the joy of Christmas-tide, but people say there is everything in a good beginning, and she may

"SHE IS A LITTLE CHRISTMAS CHILD"   Page 15.

have breathed-in unconsciously the fragrance of evergreens and holiday dinners; while the peals of sleighbells and the laughter of happy children may have fallen upon her baby ears and wakened in them a glad surprise at the merry world she had come to live in.

Her cheeks and lips were as red as holly berries; her hair was for all the world the color of a Christmas candle-flame; her eyes were bright as stars; her laugh like a chime of Christmas bells, and her tiny hands forever outstretched in giving.

Such a generous little creature you never saw! A spoonful of bread and milk had always to be taken by Mama or nurse before Carol could enjoy her supper; and whatever bit of cake or sweetmeat found its way into her pretty fingers, it was straightway broken in half and shared with Donald, Paul or Hugh; and, when they made believe nibble the morsel with affected enjoyment, she would clap her hands and crow with delight. "Why does she do it?" asked Donald, thoughtfully; "None of us boys ever did." "I hardly know," said Mama, catching her darling to her heart, "except that she is a little Christmas child, and so she has a tiny share of the blessedest birthday the world ever saw!"

II

I T was December, ten years later. Carol had seen nine Christmas trees lighted on her birthdays, one after another; nine times she had assisted in the holiday festivities of the household, though in her babyhood her share of the gayeties was somewhat limited.

For five years, certainly, she had hidden presents for Mama and Papa in their own bureau drawers, and harbored a number of secrets sufficiently large to burst a baby's brain, had it not been for the relief gained by whispering them all to Mama, at night, when she was in her crib, a proceeding which did not in the least lessen the value of a secret in her innocent mind.

For five years she had heard "'Twas the night before Christmas," and hung up a scarlet stocking many sizes too large for her, and pinned a sprig of holly on her little white night gown, to show Santa Claus that she was a "truly" Christmas child, and dreamed of furcoated saints and toy-packs and reindeer, and wished everybody a " Merry Christmas " before it was light in the morning, and lent every one of her new toys to the neighbors' children before noon, and eaten turkey and plum pudding, and gone to bed at night in a trance of happiness at the day's pleasures.

Donald was away at college now. Paul and Hugh were great manly fellows, taller than their mother. Papa Bird had grey hairs in his whiskers; and Grandma, God bless her, had been four Christmases in heaven. But Christmas in the Birds' Nest was scarcely as merry now as it used to be in the bygone years, for the little child that once brought such an added blessing to the day, lay, month after month, a patient, helpless invalid, in the room where she was born.

She had never been very strong in body, and it was with a pang of terror her mother and father noticed, soon after she was five years old, that she began to limp, ever so slightly; to complain too often of weariness, and to nestle close to her mother, saying she "would rather not go out to play, please." The illness was slight at first, and hope was always stirring in Mrs. Bird's heart. "Carol would feel stronger in the summer-time;" or, "She would be better when she had

spent a year in the country;" or, "She would outgrow
it;" or, "They would try a new physician;" but by and
by it came to be all too sure that no physician save
One could make Carol strong again, and that no
"summer-time" nor "country air," unless it were the
everlasting summer-time in a heavenly country, could
bring back the little girl to health.

The cheeks and lips that were once as red as holly-
berries faded to faint pink; the star-like eyes grew
softer, for they often gleamed through tears; and the
gay child-laugh, that had been like a chime of Christmas bells, gave place to a smile so lovely, so touching,
so tender and patient, that it filled every corner of
the house with a gentle radiance that might have come
from the face of the Christ-child himself.

Love could do nothing; and when we have said that
we have said all, for it is stronger than anything else
in the whole wide world. Mr. and Mrs. Bird were
talking it over one evening when all the children were
asleep. A famous physician had visited them that
day, and told them that sometime, it might be in one
year, it might be in more, Carol would slip quietly off
into heaven, whence she came.

"Dear heart," said Mr. Bird, pacing up and down

the library floor, "it is no use to shut our eyes to it any longer; Carol will never be well again. It almost seems as if I could not bear it when I think of that loveliest child doomed to lie there day after day, and, what is still more, to suffer pain that we are helpless to keep away from her. Merry Christmas, indeed; it gets to be the saddest day in the year to me!" and poor Mr. Bird sank into a chair by the table, and buried his face in his hands, to keep his wife from seeing the tears that would come in spite of all his efforts. "But, Donald, dear," said sweet Mrs. Bird, with trembling voice, "Christmas day may not be so merry with us as it used, but it is very happy, and that is better, and very blessed, and that is better yet. I suffer chiefly for Carol's sake, but I have almost given up being sorrowful for my own. I am too happy in the child, and I see too clearly what she has done for us and for our boys."

"That's true, bless her sweet heart," said Mr. Bird; "she has been better than a daily sermon in the house ever since she was born, and especially since she was taken ill."

"Yes, Donald and Paul and Hugh were three strong, willful, boisterous boys, but you seldom see such tenderness, devotion, thought for others and self-denial in lads of their years. A quarrel or a hot word is almost unknown in this house. Why? Carol would hear it, and it would distress her, she is so full of love and goodness. The boys study with all their might and main. Why? Partly, at least, because they like to teach Carol, and amuse her by telling her what they read. When the seamstress comes, she likes to sew in Miss Carol's room, because there she forgets her own troubles, which, Heaven knows, are sore enough! And as for me, Donald, I am a better woman every day for Carol's sake; I have to be her eyes, ears, feet, hands—her strength, her hope; and she, my own little child, is my example!"

"I was wrong, dear heart," said Mr. Bird more cheerfully; "we will try not to repine, but to rejoice instead, that we have an 'angel of the house' like Carol."

"And as for her future," Mrs. Bird went on, "I think we need not be over-anxious. I feel as if she did not belong altogether to us, and when she has done what God sent her for, He will take her back to Himself—and it may not be very long!" Here it was poor Mrs. Bird's turn to break down, and Mr. Bird's turn to comfort her.

III.

THE BIRD'S NEST.

AROL herself knew nothing of motherly tears and fatherly anxieties; she lived on peacefully in the room where she was born.

But you never would have known that room; for Mr. Bird had a great deal of money, and though he felt sometimes as if he wanted to throw it all in the ocean, since it could not buy a strong body for his little girl, yet he was glad to make the place she lived in just as beautiful as it could be made.

The room had been extended by the building of a large addition that hung out over the garden below, and was so filled with windows that it might have been a conservatory. The ones on the side were thus still nearer the little Church of our Saviour than they used to be; those in front looked out on the beautiful harbor, and those in the back commanded a view of nothing in particular but a little alley—nevertheless, they were pleasantest of all to Carol, for the Ruggles family lived in the alley, and the nine little, middle-sized and big Ruggles children were the source of inexhaustible interest.

The shutters could all be opened and Carol could take a real sun-bath in this lovely glass-house, or they could all be closed when the dear head ached or the dear eyes were tired. The carpet was of soft grey, with clusters of green bay and holly leaves. The furniture was of white wood, on which an artist had painted snow scenes and Christmas trees and groups of merry children ringing bells and singing carols.

Donald had made a pretty, polished shelf and screwed it on to the outside of the footboard, and the boys always kept this full of blooming plants, which they changed from time to time; the head-board, too, had a bracket on either side, where there were pots of maidenhair ferns.

Love-birds and canaries hung in their golden houses in the windows, and they, poor caged things, could hop as far from their wooden perches as Carol could venture from her little white bed.

On one side of the room was a bookcase filled with hundreds—yes, I mean it—with hundreds and hundreds of books; books with gay-colored pictures, books without; books with black and white outline-sketches, books with none at all; books with verses, books with stories, books that made children laugh, and some that made them cry; books with words of one syllable for tiny boys and girls, and books with words of fearful length to puzzle wise ones.

This was Carol's "Circulating Library." Every Saturday she chose ten books, jotting their names down in a little diary; into these she slipped cards that said: "Please keep this book two weeks and read it. With love, Carol Bird."

Then Mrs. Bird stepped into her carriage, and took the ten books to the Childrens' Hospital, and brought home ten others that she had left there the fortnight before.

This was a source of great happiness; for some of the Hospital children that were old enough to print or write, and were strong enough to do it, wrote Carol cunning little letters about the books, and she answered them, and they grew to be friends. (It is very funny, but you do not always have to see people to love them. Just think about it, and see if it isn't so.)

There was a high wainscoting of wood about the room, and on top of this, in a narrow gilt framework, ran a row of illuminated pictures, illustrating fairy tales, all in dull blue and gold and scarlet and silver and other lovely colors. From the door to the closet there was the story of "The Fair One with Golden Locks;" from closet to bookcase, ran "Puss in Boots;" from bookcase to fireplace, was "Jack the Giant-killer;" and on the other side of the room were "Hop o' my Thumb," "The Sleeping Beauty," and "Cinderella."

Then there was a great closet full of beautiful things to wear—but they were all dressing-gowns and slippers and shawls; and there were drawers full of toys and games; but they were such as you could play with on your lap. There were no ninepins, nor balls, nor bows and arrows, nor bean bags, nor tennis rackets; but, after all, other children needed these more than Carol Bird, for she was always happy and contented whatever she had or whatever she lacked; and after the room had been made so lovely for her, on her eighth Christmas, she always called herself, in fun, a "Bird of Paradise."

On these particular December days she was happier than usual, for Uncle Jack was coming from Europe to spend the holidays. Dear, funny, jolly, loving, wise Uncle Jack, who came every two or three years, and brought so much joy with him that the world looked as black as a thunder-cloud for a week after he went away again.

The mail had brought this letter:—

"LONDON, Nov. 28th, 188—.

Wish you merry Christmas, you dearest birdlings in America! Preen your feathers, and stretch the Birds' nest a little, if you please, and let Uncle Jack in for the holidays. I am coming with such a trunk full of treasures that you'll have to borrow the stockings of Barnum's Giant and Giantess; I am coming to squeeze a certain little lady-bird until she cries for mercy; I am coming to see if I can find a boy to take care of a little black pony I bought lately. It's the strangest thing I ever knew; I've hunted all over Europe, and can't find a boy to suit me! I'll tell you why. I've set my heart on finding one with a dimple in his chin, because this pony particularly likes dimples! ['Hurrah!' cried Hugh; 'bless my dear dimple; I'll never be ashamed of it again.'] Please drop a note to the clerk of the weather, and have a good, rousing snow-storm—say on the twenty-second. None of your meek, gentle, nonsensical, shilly-shallying snow-storms; not the sort where the flakes float lazily down from the sky as if they didn't care whether they ever got here or not, and then melt away as soon as they touch the earth, but a regular business-like whizzing, whirring, blurring, cutting snow-storm, warranted to freeze and stay on!

I should like rather a LARGE Christmas tree, if it's convenient—not one of those 'sprigs,' five or six feet high, that you used to have three or four years ago, when the birdlings were not fairly feathered out, but a tree of some size. Set it up in the garret, if necessary, and then we can cut a hole in the roof if the tree chances to be too high for the room.

Tell Bridget to begin to fatten a turkey. Tell her by the twentieth of December that turkey must not be able to stand on .ts legs for fat, and then on the next three days she must allow it to recline easily on its side, and stuff it to bursting. (One ounce of stuffing beforehand is worth a pound afterwards.)

The pudding must be unusually huge, and darkly, deeply, lugubriously black in color. It must be stuck so full of plums that the pudding itself will ooze out into the pan and not be brought on to the table at all. I expect to be there by the twentieth, to manage these little things—remembering it is the early Bird that catches the worm —but give you the instructions in case I should be delayed.

And Carol must decide on the size of the tree—she knows best, she was a Christmas child; and she must plead for the snow-storm—the 'clerk of the weather' may pay some attention to her; and she must look up the boy with the dimple for me—she's likelier to find him than I am, this minute. She must advise about the turkey, and Bridget must bring the pudding to her bedside and let her drop every separate plum into it and stir it once for luck, or I'll not eat a single slice—for Carol is the dearest part of Christmas to Uncle Jack, and he'll have none of it without her. She is better than all the turkeys and puddings and apples and spare-ribs and wreaths and garlands and mistletoe and stockings and chimneys and sleigh-bells in Christendom. She is the very sweetest Christmas Carol that was ever written, said, sung or chanted, and I am coming, as fast as ships and railway trains can carry me, to tell her so.''

Carol's joy knew no bounds. Mr. and Mrs. Bird laughed like children and kissed each other for sheer

delight, and when the boys heard it they simply
whooped like wild Indians, until the Ruggles family,
whose back yard joined their garden, gathered at the
door and wondered what was "up" in the big house.

IV.

"BIRDS OF A FEATHER FLOCK TOGETHER."

UNCLE Jack did really come on the twentieth. He was not detained by business, nor did he get left behind nor snowed up, as frequently happens in stories, and in real life too, I am afraid The snow-storm came also; and the turkey nearly died a natural and premature death from over-eating. Donald came, too; Donald, with a line of down upon his upper lip, and Greek and Latin on his tongue, and stores of knowledge in his handsome head, and stories—bless me, you couldn't turn over a chip without reminding Donald of something that happened "at College." One or the other was always at Carol's bedside, for they fancied her paler than she used to be, and they could not bear her out of sight. It was Uncle Jack, though, who sat beside her in the winter twilights. The room was quiet, and almost dark, save for the snow-light outside, and the flickering flame of the fire, that danced over

the "Sleeping Beauty's" face, and touched the Fair
One's golden locks with ruddier glory. Carol's hand
(all too thin and white these latter days) lay close
clasped in Uncle Jack's, and they talked together
quietly of many, many things. "I want to tell you
all about my plans for Christmas this year, Uncle
Jack," said Carol, on the first evening of his visit,
"because it will be the loveliest one I ever had. The
boys laugh at me for caring so much about it; but it
isn't altogether because it is Christmas nor because
it is my birthday; but long, long ago, when I first
began to be ill, I used to think, the first thing when
I waked on Christmas morning, 'To-day is Christ's
birthday ----- *and mine!*' I did not put the words
close together, because that made it seem too bold;
but I first thought, 'Christ's birthday,' and then, in
a minute, softly to myself —— '*and mine!*' 'Christ's
birthday ---- *and mine!*' And so I do not quite
feel about Christmas as other girls do. Mama says
she supposes that ever so many other children have
been born on that day. I often wonder where they
are, Uncle Jack, and whether it is a dear thought to
them, too, or whether I am so much in bed, and so
often alone, that it means more to me. Oh, I do hope

that none of them are poor, or cold, or hungry; and I wish, I wish they were all as happy as I, because they are my little brothers and sisters.   Now, Uncle Jack, dear, I am going to try and make somebody happy every single Christmas that I live, and this year it is to be the 'Ruggleses in the rear.'"

"That large and interesting brood of children in the little house at the end of the back garden?'

"Yes; isn't it nice to see so many together?   We ought to call them the Ruggles children, of course; but Donald began talking of them as the 'Ruggleses in the rear,' and Papa and Mama took it up, and now we cannot seem to help it.   The house was built for Mr. Carter's coachman, but Mr. Carter lives in Europe, and the gentleman who rents his place doesn't care what happens to it, and so this poor Irish family came to live there   When they first moved in, I used to sit in my window and watch them play in their back yard; they are so strong, and jolly, and good-natured; and then, one day, I had a terrible headache, and Donald asked them if they would please not scream quite so loud, and they explained that they were having a game of circus, but that they would change and play 'Deaf and Dumb School' all the afternoon.'

'Ha, ha, ha!" laughed Uncle Jack, "what an obliging family, to be sure."

" Yes, we all thought it very funny, and I smiled at them from the window when I was well enough to be up again. Now, Sarah Maud comes to her door when the children come home from school, and if Mama nods her head, 'Yes,' that means 'Carol is very well,' and then you ought to hear the little Ruggleses yell —I believe they try to see how much noise they can make; but if Mama shakes her head, 'No,' they always play at quiet games. Then, one day, 'Cary,' my pet canary, flew out of her cage, and Peter Ruggles caught her and brought her back, and I had him up here in my room to thank him."

"Is Peter the oldest?"

"No; Sarah Maud is the oldest—she helps do the washing; and Peter is the next. He is a dressmaker's boy."

" And which is the pretty little red-haired girl? "

" That's Kitty."

" And the fat youngster? "

" Baby Larry."

" And that freckled one? "

"Now, don't laugh—that's Peoria!"

"Carol, you are joking."

"No, really, Uncle dear. She was born in Peoria; that's all."

"And is the next boy Oshkosh?"

"No," laughed Carol, "the others are Susan, and Clement, and Eily, and Cornelius."

"How did you ever learn all their names?"

"Well, I have what I call a 'window-school.' It is too cold now; but in warm weather I am wheeled out on my little balcony, and the Ruggleses climb up and walk along our garden fence, and sit down on the roof of our carriage-house. That brings them quite near, and I read to them and tell them stories; On Thanksgiving Day they came up for a few minutes, it was quite warm at eleven o'clock, and we told each other what we had to be thankful for; but they gave such queer answers that Papa had to run away for fear of laughing; and I couldn't understand them very well. Susan was thankful for '*trunks*,' of all things in the world; Cornelius, for 'horse cars;' Kitty, for 'pork steak;' while Clem, who is very quiet, brightened up when I came to him, and said he was thankful for '*his lame puppy*.' Wasn't that pretty?"

"It might teach some of us a lesson, mightn't it, little girl?"

"That's what Mama said. Now I'm going to give this whole Christmas to the Ruggleses; and, Uncle Jack, I earned part of the money myself."

"You, my bird; how?"

"Well, you see, it could not be my own, own Christmas if Papa gave me all the money, and I thought to really keep Christ's birthday I ought to do something of my very own; and so I talked with Mama. Of course she thought of something lovely; she always does; Mama's head is just brimming over with lovely thoughts, and all I have to do is ask, and out pops the very one I want. This thought was, to let her write down, just as I told her, a description of how a little girl lived in her own room three years, and what she did to amuse herself; and we sent it to a magazine and got twenty-five dollars for it. Just think!"

"Well, well," cried Uncle Jack, "my little girl a real author! And what are you going to do with this wonderful 'own' money of yours?"

"I shall give the nine Ruggleses a grand Christmas dinner here in this very room—that will be Papa's contribution, and afterwards a beautiful Christmas tree, fairly blooming with presents—that will be my part; for I have another way of adding to my twenty-five dollars, so that I can buy everything I like. I should like it very much if you would sit at the head of the table, Uncle Jack, for nobody could ever be frightened of you, you dearest, dearest, dearest thing that ever was! Mama is going to help us, but Papa and the boys are going to eat together down stairs for fear of making the little Ruggleses shy; and after we've had a merry time with the tree we can open my window and all listen together to the music at the evening church-service, if it comes before the children go. I have written a letter to the organist, and asked him if I might have the two songs I like best. Will you see if it is all right?"

"BIRDS' NEST, Dec. 21st, 188—.

DEAR MR. WILKIE,—I am the little sick girl who lives next door to the church, and, as I seldom go out, the music on practice days and Sundays is one of my greatest pleasures.

I want to know if you can let the boys sing 'Carol, brothers, carol,' on Christmas night, and if the one who sings 'My ain countree' so beautifully may please sing that too. I think it is the loveliest song in the world, but it always makes me cry; does'nt it you?

If it isn't too much trouble, I hope they can sing them both quite early, as after ten o'clock I may be asleep. —Yours respectfully,

CAROL BIRD.

P.S.—The reason I like 'Carol, brothers, carol,' is because the choir-boys sang it eleven years ago, the morning I was born, and put it into Mama's head to call me Carol. She didn't remember then that my other name would be Bird, because she was half asleep, and couldn't think of but one thing at a time. Donald says if I had been born on the Fourth of July they would have named me 'Independence,' or if on the twenty-second of February, 'Georgina,' or even 'Cherry,' like Cherry in Martin Chuzzlewit; but I like my own name and birthday best.—Yours truly,

CAROL BIRD.''

Uncle Jack thought the letter quite right, and did not even smile at her telling the organist so many family items. The days flew by, as they always fly in holiday time, and it was Christmas eve before anybody knew it. The family festival was quiet and very pleasant, but quite swallowed up in the grander preparations for next day. Carol and Elfrida, her pretty German nurse, had ransacked books, and introduced so many plans, and plays, and customs and merry-makings from Germany, and Holland, and England and a dozen other places, that you would scarcely have known how or where you were keeping Christmas. The dog and the cat had enjoyed their celebration under Carol's direction. Each had a tiny table with a lighted candle in the center, and a bit of Bologna sausage placed very near it, and everybody laughed till the tears stood in their eyes to see Villikins and

Dinah struggle to nibble the sausages, and at the same
time evade the candle flame. Villikins barked, and
sniffed, and howled in impatience, and after many vain
attempts succeeded in dragging off the prize, though
he singed his nose in doing it. Dinah, meanwhile,
watched him placidly, her delicate nostrils quivering
with expectation, and, after all excitement had subsided, walked with dignity to the table, her beautiful
gray satin trail sweeping behind her, and, calmly
putting up one velvet paw, drew the sausage gently
down, and walked out of the room without "turning a
hair," so to speak. Elfrida had scattered handfuls of
seeds over the snow in the garden, that the wild birds
might have a comfortable breakfast next morning, and
had stuffed bundles of dried grasses in the fireplaces,
so that the reindeer of Santa Claus could refresh themselves after their long gallops across country. This
was really only done for fun, but it pleased Carol.

And when, after dinner, the whole family had gone
to church to see the Christmas decorations, Carol
limped wearily out on her little crutches, and, with
Elfrida's help, placed all the family boots in a row in
the upper hall. That was to keep the dear ones from
quarreling all through the year. There were Papa's

stout top boots; Mama's pretty buttoned shoes next; then Uncle Jack's, Donald's, Paul's and Hugh's; and at the end of the line her own little white worsted slippers. Last, and sweetest of all, like the little children in Austria, she put a lighted candle in her window to guide the dear Christ-child, lest he should stumble in the dark night as he passed up the deserted street. This done, she dropped into bed, a rather tired, but very happy Christmas fairy.

V.

BEFORE the earliest Ruggles could wake and toot his five-cent tin horn, Mrs. Ruggles was up and stirring about the house, for it was a gala day in the family. Gala day! I should think so! Were not her nine "childern" invited to a dinner-party at the great house, and weren't they going to sit down free and equal with the mightiest in the land? She had been preparing for this grand occasion ever since the receipt of the invitation, which, by the way, had been speedily enshrined in an old photograph frame and hung under the looking-glass in the most prominent place in the kitchen, where it stared the occasional visitor directly in the eye, and made him pale with envy:

"BIRDS' NEST, Dec. 17th, 188—.

DEAR MRS. RUGGLES,—I am going to have a dinner-party on Christmas day, and would like to have all your children come. I want them every one, please, from Sarah Maud to Baby Larry. Mama says dinner will be at half-past five, and the Christmas tree at seven; so you may expect them home at nine o'clock. Wishing you a Merry Christmas and a Happy New Year, I am, yours truly,

CAROL BIRD.''

Breakfast was on the table promptly at seven o'clock, and there was very little of it, too; for it was an excellent day for short rations, though Mrs. Ruggles heaved a sigh as she reflected that even the boys, with their India-rubber stomachs, would be just as hungry the day after the dinner-party as if they had never had any at all.

As soon as the scanty meal was over, she announced the plan of the campaign: "Now Susan, you an' Kitty wash up the dishes; an' Peter, can't you spread up the beds, so't I can git ter cuttin' out Larry's new suit? I aint satisfied with his close, an' I thought in the night of a way to make him a dress out of my old plaid shawl—kind o' Scotch style, yer know. You other boys clear out from under foot! Clem, you and Con hop into bed with Larry while I wash yer underflannins; 'twont take long to dry 'em. Sarah Maud, I think 'twould be perfeckly han'som if you ripped them brass buttons off yer uncle's policeman's coat an' sewed 'em in a row up the front o' yer green skirt. Susan, you must iron out yours an' Kitty's apurns; an' there, I came mighty near forgettin' Peory's stockin's! I counted the whole lot last night when I was washin' of 'em, an' there aint but nineteen anyhow yer fix 'em, an' no nine pairs mates nohow; an' I aint goin' ter have my childern wear odd stockin's to a dinner-comp'ny, brought up as I was! Eily, can't you run out and ask Mis' Cullen ter lend me a pair o' stockin's for Peory, an tell her if she will, Peory 'll give Jim half her candy when she gets home. Wont yer, Peory?"

Peoria was young and greedy, and thought the remedy so much worse than the disease that she set up a deafening howl at the projected bargain—a howl so rebellious and so out of all season that her mother started in her direction with flashing eye and uplifted hand; but she let it fall suddenly, saying, "No, I wont lick ye Christmas day, if yer drive me crazy; but speak up smart, now, 'n say whether yer'd ruther give Tim Cullen half yer candy or go bare-legged ter the party?" The matter being put so plainly, Peoria collected her faculties, dried her tears and chose the lesser evil, Clem having hastened the decision by an affectionate wink, that meant he'd go halves with her on his candy.

"That's a lady;" cried her mother. "Now, you

young ones that aint doin' nothin', play all yer want ter
before noontime, for after ye git through eatin' at
twelve o'clock me 'n Sarah Maud's goin' ter give yer
such a washin' an' combin' an' dressin' as yer never had
before an' never will agin, an' then I'm goin to set yer
down an' give yer two solid hours trainin' in manners;
an' 'twont be no foolin' neither."

"All we've got ter do 's go eat!" grumbled Peter.

"Well, that's enough," responded his mother;
"there's more 'n one way of eatin', let me tell yer, an'
you've got a heap ter learn about it, Peter Ruggles.
Lord sakes, I wish you childern could see the way I
was fetched up to eat—never took a meal o' vittles in
the kitchen before I married Ruggles; but yer can't
keep up that style with nine young ones 'n yer Pa
always off ter sea."

The big Ruggleses worked so well, and the little
Ruggleses kept from "under foot" so successfully,
that by one o'clock nine complete toilets were laid
out in solemn grandeur on the beds. I say, "complete;" but I do not know whether they would be
called so in the best society. The law of compen-
sation had been well applied; he that had necktie
had no cuffs; she that had sash had no handkerchief,

and *vice versa;* but they all had boots and a certain amount of clothing, such as it was, the outside layer being in every case quite above criticism.

"Now, Sarah Maud," said Mrs. Ruggles, her face shining with excitement, "everything is red up an' we can begin. I've got a boiler 'n a kettle 'n a pot o' hot water. Peter, you go into the back bedroom, an' I'll take Susan, Kitty, Peory an' Cornelius; an' Sarah Maud, you take Clem, n' Eily, n' Larry, one to a time, an' git as fur as you can with 'em, an' then I'll finish 'em off while you do yerself."

Sarah Maud couldn't have scrubbed with any more decision and force if she had been doing floors, and the little Ruggleses bore it bravely, not from natural heroism, but for the joy that was set before them. Not being satisfied, however, with the "tone" of their complexions, she wound up operations by applying a little Bristol brick from the knife-board, which served as the proverbial "last straw," from under which the little Ruggleses issued rather red and raw and out of temper. When the clock struck three they were all clothed, and most of them in their right minds, ready for those last touches that always take the most time. Kitty's red hair was curled in thirty-four ringlets,

Sarah Maud's was braided in one pig-tail, and Susan's
and Eily's in two braids apiece, while Peoria's resisted
all advances in the shape of hair oils and stuck out
straight on all sides, like that of the Circassian girl of
the circus—so Clem said; and he was sent into the
bed-room for it too, from whence he was dragged out
forgivingly by Peoria herself, five minutes later.   Then
—exciting moment—came linen collars for some and
neckties and bows for others, and Eureka! the Ruggleses were dressed, and Solomon in all his glory was not
arrayed like one of these!   A row of seats was formed
directly through the middle of the kitchen.   There
were not quite chairs enough for ten, since the family
had rarely all wanted to sit down at once, sombody
always being out, or in bed, but the wood box and the
coal-hod finished out the line nicely.   The children
took their places according to age, Sarah Maud at the
head and Larry on the coal-hod, and Mrs. Ruggles
seated herself in front, surveying them proudly as she
wiped the sweat of honest toil from her brow.

"Well," she exclaimed, "if I do say so as shouldn't,
I never see a cleaner, more stylish mess o' childern in
my life! I do wish Ruggles could look at ye for a
minute! Now, I've of'en told ye what kind of a fam-

ily the McGrills was. I've got some reason to be proud;
your uncle is on the po-lice force o' New York city;
you can take up the newspaper most any day an' see
his name printed right out—James McGrill, and I can't
have my childern fetched up common, like some folks.
When they go out they've got to have close, and learn
ter act decent! Now, I want ter see how yer goin' to
behave when yer git there to-night. Lets start in at
the beginnin' 'n act out the whole business. Pile into
the bed-room, there, every last one of ye, an' show me
how yer goin' ter go in't the parlor. This'll be the
parlor 'n I'll be Mis' Bird." The youngsters hustled
into the next room in high glee, and Mrs. Ruggles
drew herself up in her chair with an infinitely haughty
and purse-proud expression that much better suited a
descendant of the McGrills than modest Mrs. Bird.
The bed-room was small, and there presently ensued
such a clatter that you would have thought a herd of
wild cattle had broken loose; the door opened, and
they straggled in, all the little ones giggling, with
Sarah Maud at the head, looking as if she had been
caught in the act of stealing sheep; while Larry, being
last in line, seemed to think the door a sort of gate of
heaven which would be shut in his face if he didn't get

"I WANT TER SEE HOW YER GOIN' TO BEHAVE."   Page 44.

there in time; accordingly he struggled ahead of his elders and disgraced himself by tumbling in head foremost.

Mrs. Ruggles looked severe. "There, I knew yer'd do it in some sech fool-way,—try it agin 'n if Larry can't come in on two legs he can stay ter home!"

The matter began to assume a graver aspect; the little Ruggleses stopped giggling and backed into the bed-room, issuing presently with lock step, Indian file, a scared and hunted expression in every countenance.

"No, no, no!" cried Mrs. Ruggles, in despair; "Yer look for all the world like a gang o' pris'ners; there aint no style ter that; spread out more, can't yer, an' act kind o' careless like—nobody's goin' ter kill ye!" The third time brought deserved success, and the pupils took their seats in the row. "Now, yer know," said Mrs. Ruggles, "there aint enough decent hats to go round, an' if there was I don' know 's I'd let yer wear 'em, for the boys would never think to take 'em off when they got inside—but, anyhow, there aint enough good ones. Now, look me in the eye. You need'nt wear no hats, none of yer, an' when yer get int' the parlor 'n they ask yer ter lay off yer hats, Sarah Maud must speak up an' say it was sech a pleasant evenin' an' sech a short walk that you left yer hats to home to save trouble. Now, can you remember?"

All the little Ruggleses shouted, "Yes, marm," in chorus.

"What have you got ter do with it," demanded their mother; "did I tell *you* to say it! Wasn't I talkin' ter Sarah Maud?" The little Ruggleses hung their diminished heads. "Yes, marm," they piped, more feebly. "Now git up, all of ye, an' try it. Speak up, Sarah Maud."

Sarah Maud's tongue clove to the roof of her mouth.

"Quick!"

"Ma thought—it was—sech a pleasant hat that we'd —we'd better leave our short walk to home," recited Sarah Maud, in an agony of mental effort.

This was too much for the boys.

"Oh, whatever shall I do with ye?" moaned the unhappy mother; "I suppose I've got to learn it to yer!" which she did, word for word, until Sarah Maud thought she could stand on her head and say it backwards.

"Now, Cornelius, what are *you* goin' ter say ter make yerself good comp'ny?"

"Dunno!" said Cornelius, turning pale.

"Well, ye ain't goin' to set there like a bump on a log 'thout sayin' a word ter pay for yer vittles, air ye? Ask Mis' Bird how she's feelin' this evenin', or if Mr. Bird's havin' a busy season, or somethin' like that. Now we'll make b'lieve we've got ter the dinner—that won't be so hard, 'cause yer'll have somethin' to do—its awful bothersome ter stan' round an' act stylish. If they have napkins, Sarah Maud down to Peory may put 'em in their laps 'n the rest of ye can tuck 'em in yer necks. Don't eat with yer fingers—don't grab no vittles off one 'nothers plates; don't reach out for nothin', but wait till yer asked, 'n if yer never *git* asked don't git up and grab it—don't spill nothin' on the table cloth, or like's not Mis' Bird 'll send yer away from the table. Now we'll try a few things ter see how they'll go! Mr. Clement, do you eat cramb'ry sarse?"

"Bet yer life!" cried Clem, who, not having taken in the idea exactly, had mistaken this for an ordinary family question.

"Clement Ruggles, do you mean to tell me that you'd say that to a dinner party? I'll give ye one more chance. Mr. Clement, will you take some of the cramb'ry?"

"Yes marm, thank ye kindly, if you happen ter have any handy."

"Very good, indeed! Mr. Peter, do you speak for white or dark meat?"

"I ain't particler as ter color—anything that nobody else wants will suit me," answered Peter with his best air.

"First rate! nobody could speak more genteel than that. Miss Kitty, will you have hard or soft sarse with your pudden?"

"A little of both if you please, an' I'm much obliged," said Kitty with decided ease and grace, at which all the other Ruggleses pointed the finger of shame at her and Peter *grunted* expressively, that their meaning might not be mistaken.

"You just stop your gruntin', Peter Ruggles; that was all right. I wish I could git it inter your heads that it aint so much what yer say, as the way yer say it. Eily, you an' Larry's too little to train, so you just look at the rest, an' do 's they do, an' the Lord have mercy on ye an' help ye to act decent! Now, is there anything more ye'd like to practice?"

"If yer tell me one more thing I can't set up an' eat," said Peter, gloomily; "I'm so cram full o' manners now I'm ready ter bust 'thout no dinner at all."

"Me too," chimed in Cornelius.

"Well, I'm sorry for yer both," rejoined Mrs. Ruggles, sarcastically; "if the 'mount o' manners yer've got on hand now, troubles ye, you're dreadful easy hurt! Now, Sarah Maud, after dinner, about once in so often, you must say, 'I guess we'd better be goin';' an' if they say, 'Oh, no, set a while longer,' yer can stay; but if they don't say nothin' you've got ter get up an' go. Can you remember?"

"*About once in so often!*" Could any words in the language be fraught with more terrible and wearing uncertainty?

"Well," answered Sarah Maud, mournfully, "seems as if this whole dinner party set right square on top o' me! Maybe I could manage my own manners, but ter manage nine mannerses is worse 'n staying to home!"

"Oh, don't fret," said her mother, good naturedly, "I guess you'll git along. I wouldn't mind if folks would only say, 'Oh, childern will be childern;' but they won't. They'll say, 'Land o' Goodness, who fetched them childern up?' Now its quarter past five; you can go, an' whatever yer do, don't forget your mother was a McGrill!"

VI.

HE children went out the back door quietly, and were presently lost to sight, Sarah Maud slipping and stumbling along absent-mindedly as she recited, under her breath, "It-was-such-a pleasant· evenin'-an-sech-a-short-walk-we-thought-we'd-leave-our-hats-to-home."

Peter rang the door bell, and presently a servant admitted them, and, whispering something in Sarah's ear, drew her downstairs into the kitchen. The other Ruggleses stood in horror-stricken groups as the door closed behind their commanding officer; but there was no time for reflection, for a voice from above was heard, saying, "Come right up stairs, please!"

> "Theirs not to make reply,
> Theirs not to reason why,
> Theirs but to do or die."

Accordingly, they walked upstairs, and Elfrida, the

nurse, ushered them into a room more splendid than anything they had ever seen. But, oh woe! where was Sarah Maud! and was it Fate that Mrs. Bird should say, at once, "Did you lay your hats in the hall?" Peter felt himself elected by circumstance the head of the family, and, casting one imploring look at tongue-tied Susan, standing next him, said huskily, "It was so very pleasant—that—that——" "That we hadn't good hats enough to go round," put in little Susan, bravely, to help him out, and then froze with horror that the ill-fated words had slipped off her tongue.

However, Mrs. Bird said, pleasantly, "Of course you wouldn't wear hats such a short distance—I forgot when I asked. Now, will you come right in to Miss Carol's room, she is so anxious to see you?"

Just then Sarah Maud came up the back-stairs, so radiant with joy from her secret interview with the cook, that Peter could have pinched her with a clear conscience, and Carol gave them a joyful welcome. "But where is Baby Larry?" she cried, looking over the group with searching eye. "Didn't he come?"

"Larry! Larry!" Good Gracious, where was Larry? They were all sure that he had come in with them, for Susan remembered scolding him for tripping over the door-mat. Uncle Jack went into convulsions of laughter. "Are you sure there were nine of you?" he asked, merrily.

"I think so, sir," said Peoria, timidly; "but, anyhow, there was Larry;" and she showed signs of weeping.

"Oh, well, cheer up!" cried Uncle Jack. "I guess he's not lost—only mislaid. I'll go and find him before you can say Jack Robinson!"

"I'll go, too, if you please, sir," said Sarah Maud, "for it was my place to mind him, an' if he's lost I can't relish my vittles!"

The other Ruggleses stood rooted to the floor. Was this a dinner party, forsooth; and, if so, why were such things ever spoken of as festive occasions?

Sarah Maud went out through the hall, calling, "Larry! Larry!" and without any interval of suspense a thin voice piped up from below, "Here I be!" The truth was that Larry, being deserted by his natural guardian, dropped behind the rest, and wriggled into the hat-tree to wait for her, having no notion of walking unprotected into the jaws of a dinner-party. Finding that she did not come, he tried to crawl from his refuge and call somebody, when—dark and dreadful

ending to a tragic day—he found that he was too much
intertwined with umbrellas and canes to move a single
step. He was afraid to yell! When I have said this
of Larry Ruggles I have pictured a state of helpless
terror that ought to wring tears from every eye; and
the sound of Sarah Maud's beloved voice, some seconds
later, was like a strain of angel music in his ears.
Uncle Jack dried his tears, carried him upstairs, and
soon had him in breathless fits of laughter, while Carol
so made the other Ruggleses forget themselves that they
were soon talking like accomplished diners-out.

Carol's bed had been moved into the farthest corner
of the room, and she was lying on the outside, dressed
in a wonderful soft white wrapper. Her golden hair
fell in soft fluffy curls over her white forehead and
neck, her cheeks flushed delicately, her eyes beamed
with joy, and the children told their mother, afterwards, that she looked as beautiful as the pictures of
the Blessed Virgin. There was great bustle behind a
huge screen in another part of the room, and at half-
past five this was taken away, and the Christmas dinner-
table stood revealed. What a wonderful sight it was
to the poor little Ruggles children, who ate their sometimes scanty meals on the kitchen table! It blazed

with tall colored candles, it gleamed with glass and
silver, it blushed with flowers, it groaned with good
things to eat; so it was not strange that the Ruggleses, forgetting that their mother was a McGrill,
shrieked in admiration of the fairy spectacle. But
Larry's behavior was the most disgraceful, for he
stood not upon the order of his going, but went at
once for a high chair that pointed unmistakably to him,
climbed up like a squirrel, gave a comprehensive look
at the turkey, clapped his hands in ecstacy, rested his
fat arms on the table, and cried, with joy, "I beat the
hull lot o' yer!"   Carol laughed until she cried, giving
orders, meanwhile, "Uncle Jack, please sit at the
head, Sarah Maud at the foot, and that will leave four
on each side; Mama is going to help Elfrida, so that
the children need not look after each other, but just
have a good time."

A sprig of holly lay by each plate, and nothing
would do but each little Ruggles must leave his
seat and have it pinned on by Carol, and as each
course was served one of them pleaded to take something to her.   There was hurrying to and fro, I
can assure you, for it is quite a difficult matter to serve
a Christmas dinner on the third floor of a great city

"THE RUGGLESES NEVER FORGOT IT." Page 55.

house; but if every dish had had to be carried up a rope ladder the servants would gladly have done so. There was turkey and chicken, with delicious gravy and stuffing, and there were half-a-dozen vegetables, with cranberry jelly, and celery, and pickles; and as for the way these delicacies were served, the Ruggleses never forgot it as long as they lived.

Peter nudged Kitty, who sat next him, and said, "Look, will yer, ev'ry feller's got his own partic'lar butter; I suppose that's to show yer can eat that much 'n no more. No, it ain't neither, for that pig of a Peory's just gittin' another helpin'!" "Yes," whispered Kitty, "an' the napkins is marked with big red letters. I wonder if that's so nobody 'll nip 'em; an' oh, Peter, look at the pictures painted right on ter the dishes. Did yer ever!"

"The plums is all took out o' my cramb'ry sarse, an' it's friz to a stiff jell!" shouted Peoria, in wild excitement.

"Hi—yah! I got a wish-bone!" sung Larry, regardless of Sarah Maud's frown; after which she asked to have his seat changed, giving as excuse that he gen'ally set beside her, an' would "feel strange;" the true reason being that she desired to kick him gently, under the table, whenever he passed what might be termed "the McGrill line."

"I declare to goodness," murmured Susan, on the other side, "there's so much to look at I can't scarcely eat nothin'!"

"Bet yer life I can!" said Peter, who had kept one servant busily employed ever since he sat down; for, luckily, no one was asked by Uncle Jack whether he would have a second helping, but the dishes were quietly passed under their noses, and not a single Ruggles refused anything that was offered him, even unto the seventh time. Then, when Carol and Uncle Jack perceived that more turkey was a physical impossibility, the meats were taken off and the dessert was brought in— a dessert that would have frightened a strong man after such a dinner as had preceded it. Not so the Ruggleses—for a strong man is nothing to a small boy—and they kindled to the dessert as if the turkey had been a dream and the six vegetables an optical delusion. There was plum-pudding, mince-pie, and ice-cream, and there were nuts, and raisins, and oranges. Kitty chose ice-cream, explaining that she knew it " by sight," but hadn't never tasted none; but all the rest took the entire variety, without any regard to consequences.

"My dear child," whispered Uncle Jack, as he took Carol an orange, "there is no doubt about the necessity of this feast, but I do advise you after this to have them twice a year, or quarterly, perhaps, for the way they eat is positively dangerous; I assure you I tremble for that terrible Peoria. I'm going to run races with her after dinner."

"Never mind," laughed Carol, "let them eat for once; it does my heart good to see them, and they shall come oftener next year."

The feast being over, the Ruggleses lay back in their chairs languidly, and the table was cleared in a trice; then a door was opened into the next room, and there, in a corner facing Carol's bed, which had been wheeled as close as possible, stood the brilliantly lighted Christmas-tree, glittering with gilded walnuts and tiny silver balloons, and wreathed with snowy chains of pop-corn. The presents had been bought mostly with Carol's story money, and were selected after long consultations with Mrs. Bird. Each girl had a blue knitted hood, and each boy a red crocheted comforter, all made by Mama, Carol and Elfrida (" because if you buy everything, it doesn't show so much love," said Carol). Then every girl had a pretty plaid dress of a different color, and every boy a warm coat of the right size. Here the useful presents stopped, and they were quite enough; but Carol had pleaded to give them something "for fun." "I know they need the clothes," she had said, when they were talking over the matter just after Thanksgiving, "but they don't care much for them, after all. Now, Papa, won't you *please* let me go without part of my presents this year, and give me the money they would cost, to buy something to amuse them?"

"You can have both," said Mr. Bird, promptly; "is there any need of my little girl's going without her Christmas, I should like to know? Spend all the money you like."

"But that isn't the thing," objected Carol, nestling close to her father; "it wouldn't be mine. What is the use? Haven't I almost everything already, and am I not the happiest girl in the world this year, with Uncle Jack and Donald at home? Now, Papa, you know very well it is more blessed to give than to receive; then why won't you let me do it? You never look half as happy when you are getting your presents as when you are giving us ours. Now, Papa, submit, or I shall have to be very firm and disagreeable with you!"

"Very well, your Highness, I surrender."

"That's a dear Papa! Now, what were you going to give me? Confess!"

"A bronze figure of Santa Claus; and in the little round belly, that shakes, when he laughs, like a bowl full of jelly, is a wonderful clock. Oh, you would never give it up if you could see it."

"Nonsense," laughed Carol; "as I never have to get up to breakfast, nor go to bed, nor catch trains, I think my old clock will do very well! Now, Mama, what were you going to give me?"

"Oh, I hadn't decided. A few more books, and a gold thimble, and a smelling-bottle, and a music-box."

"Poor Carol," laughed the child, merrily, "she can afford to give up these lovely things, for there will still be left Uncle Jack, and Donald, and Paul, and Hugh, and Uncle Rob, and Aunt Elsie, and a dozen other people."

So Carol had her way, as she generally did, but it was usually a good way, which was fortunate, under the circumstances; and Sarah Maud had a set of Miss Alcott's books, and Peter a modest silver watch, Cornelius a tool-chest, Clement a dog-house for his "lame puppy," Larry a magnificent Noah's ark, and each of the little girls a beautiful doll. You can well believe that everybody was very merry and very thankful. All the family, from Mr. Bird down to the cook, said they had never seen so much happiness in the space of three hours; but it had to end, as all things do. The candles flickered and went out, the tree was left alone with its gilded ornaments, and Mrs. Bird sent the children down stairs at half-past eight, thinking that Carol looked tired.

"Now, my darling, you have done quite enough for one day," said Mrs. Bird, getting Carol into her little night-dress; "I am afraid you will feel worse to-morrow, and that would be a sad ending to such a good time."

"Oh, wasn't it a lovely, lovely time," sighed Carol. "From first to last, everything was just right. I shall never forget Larry's face when he looked at the turkey; nor Peter's, when he saw his watch; nor that sweet, sweet Kitty's smile when she kissed her dolly; nor the tears in poor, dull Sarah Maud's eyes when she thanked me for her books; nor ——"

"But we mustn't talk any longer about it to-night," said Mrs. Bird, anxiously; "you are too tired, dear."

"I am not so very tired, Mama. I have felt well all

day; not a bit of pain anywhere. Perhaps this has done me good."

"Perhaps; I hope so. There was no noise or confusion; it was just a merry time. Now, may I close the door and leave you alone? I will steal in softly the first thing in the morning, and see if you are all right; but I think you need to be quiet."

"Oh, I'm willing to stay alone; but I am not sleepy yet, and I am going to hear the music by and by, you know."

"Yes, I have opened the window a little, and put the screen in front of it, so that you will not feel the air."

"Can I have the shutters open; and won't you turn my bed a little, please? This morning I woke ever so early, and one bright beautiful star shone in that eastern window. I never saw it before, and I thought of the Star in the East, that guided the wise men to the place where Jesus was. Good night, Mama. Such a happy, happy day!"

"Good night, my precious little Christmas Carol— mother's blessed Christmas child."

"Bend your head a minute, mother dear," whispered Carol, calling her mother back. "Mama, dear, I do think that we have kept Christ's birthday this time just as He would like it.   Don't you?"

"I am sure of it," said Mrs. Bird, softly.

VII.

THE BIRDLING FLIES AWAY.

HE Ruggleses had finished a last romp in the library with Paul and Hugh, and Uncle Jack had taken them home, and stayed a while to chat with Mrs. Ruggles, who opened the door for them, her face all aglow with excitement and delight. When Kitty and Clem showed her the oranges and nuts they had kept for her, she astonished them by saying that at six o'clock Mrs. Bird had sent her in the finest dinner she had ever seen in her life; and not only that, but a piece of dress-goods that must have cost a dollar a yard if it cost a cent. As Uncle Jack went down the little porch he looked back into the window for a last glimpse of the family, as the children gathered about their mother, showing their beautiful presents again and again, and then upward to a window in the great house yonder. "A little child shall lead them," he thought; "well, if—— if anything ever happens to Carol, I will take the Ruggleses under my wing."

"Softly, Uncle Jack," whispered the boys, as he walked into the library a little while later; "We are listening to the music in the church. They sang 'Carol, brothers, carol,' a while ago, and now we think the organist is beginning to play 'My ain countree' for Carol."

"I hope she hears it," said Mrs. Bird; "but they are very late to-night, and I dare not speak to her, lest she should be asleep. It is after ten o'clock "

The boy-soprano, clad in white surplice, stood in the organ loft. The lamps shone full upon his crown of fair hair, and his pale face, with its serious blue eyes, looked paler than usual. Perhaps it was something in the tender thrill of the voice, or in the sweet words, but there were tears in many eyes, both in the church and in the great house next door.

> " I am far frae my hame,
>   I am weary aften whiles
> For the langed for hame-bringin
>   An' my Faether's welcome smiles
> An' I'll ne'er be fu' content,
>   Until my e'en do see
> The gowden gates o' heaven
>   In my ain countree.

"MY AIN COUNTREE." Page 64.

The earth is decked wi' flow'rs,
　Mony tinted, fresh an' gay,
An' the birdies warble blythely,
　For my Faether made them sae;
But these sights an' these soun's
　Will as naething be to me,
When I hear the angels singin'
　In my ain countree.

Like a bairn to its mither.
　A wee birdie to its nest,
I fain would be gangin' noo
　Unto my Faether's breast;
For He gathers in His arms
　Helpless, worthless lambs like me,
An' carries them Himsel'
　To His ain countree."

There were tears in many eyes, but not in Carol's. The loving heart had quietly ceased to beat and the "wee birdie" in the great house had flown to its "home nest." Carol had fallen asleep! But as to the song, I think perhaps, I cannot say, she heard it after all!

　*　*　*　*　*　*　*　*　*

So sad an ending to a happy day! Perhaps—to those who were left—and yet Carol's mother, even in the freshness of her grief, was glad that her darling had slipped away on the loveliest day of her life, out of its glad content, into everlasting peace.

She was glad that she had gone, as she had come, on wings of song, when all the world was brimming over with joy; glad of every grateful smile, of every joyous burst of laughter, of every loving thought and word and deed the dear, last day had brought.

Sadness reigned, it is true, in the little house behind the garden; and one day poor Sarah Maud, with a courage born of despair, threw on her hood and shawl, walked straight to a certain house a mile away, dashed up the marble steps and into good Dr. Bartol's office, falling at his feet as she cried, "Oh, sir, it was me an' our childern that went to Miss Carol's last dinner party, an' if we made her worse we can't never be happy again!" Then the kind old gentleman took her rough hand in his and told her to dry her tears, for neither she nor any of her flock had hastened Carol's flight—indeed, he said that had it not been for the strong hopes and wishes that filled her tired heart, she could not have stayed long enough to keep that last merry Christmas with her dear ones.

And so the old years, fraught with memories, die, one after another, and the new years, bright with hopes, are born to take their places; but Carol lives again in every chime of Christmas bells that peal glad tidings and in every Christmas anthem sung by childish voices.